THEODORE TOO
and the Too-long Nap

by Michelle Mulder
illustrated by Yolanda Poplawska

NIMBUS
PUBLISHING

Nimbus Publishing Limited

PO Box 9166

Halifax, NS   B3K 5M8

(902) 455-4286

Printed and bound in Canada

Design: Heather Bryan

Library and Archives Canada Cataloguing in Publication

Mulder, Michelle

Theodore Too and the too-long nap / Michelle Mulder; with illustrations by Yolanda Poplawska.

ISBN 1-55109-571-8

I. Poplawska, Yolanda   II. Title.

PS8626.U435T48 2006   jC813'.6   C2006-901564-3

We acknowledge the financial support of the Government of Canada through the Book Publishing Industry Development Program (BPIDP) and the Canada Council, and of the Province of Nova Scotia through the Department of Tourism, Culture and Heritage for our publishing activities.

Today was Theodore Too's birthday. The sun shone brightly, and Theodore Too chugged excitedly around Halifax Harbour. Fisherman Murphy waved from his restaurant, and Dartmouth Ferry blew her horn.

This afternoon, all of Theodore Too's friends
would gather to eat cake and sing and play games
until the sun went down.

"Cruise ship Gerta arrived early this morning," said Lucy Tug. "She came all the way from Germany for your party."

Theodore Too gave a long, low toot of his horn. "She must be really tired. I'll go welcome her."

The young tug hurried off, smiling to tourists on the boardwalk who waved as he passed. George Lighthouse winked from the edge of his island. "Happy birthday!"

Guy Seagull flew overhead just as Theodore Too spotted McNab's Island.

"Happy ice cream day!" Guy called.

Theodore Too laughed. "You've been dreaming of ice cream ever since I told you about the party."

"Of course," Guy said. "Seagulls don't get dessert very often."

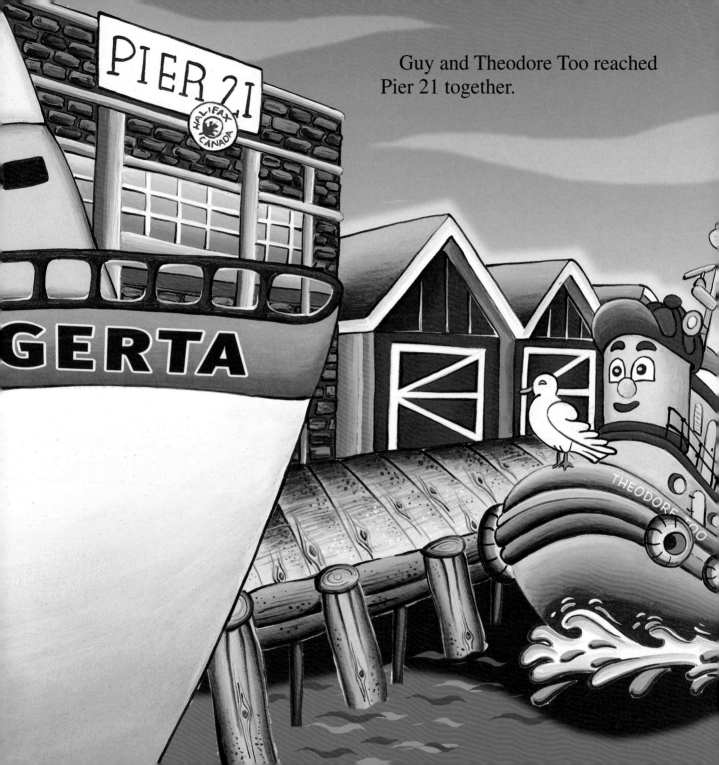

Guy and Theodore Too reached
Pier 21 together.

"There's Gerta," Theodore Too said, and smiled at a big white ship with a three-colour flag. "She travelled all week to get here for my party, and she must have really needed a nap."

"It looks like she's still sleeping," said Guy.

The seagull was right. The big white ship was in a deep sleep. Theodore Too gave a toot of his horn, but—*hup-hup-hup brrrrrr*—the ship kept snoring.

GERTA

THEODORE TOO

GERTA

THEODORE TOO

Guy called a few times, and Theodore Too raced around, tooting louder. "If she sleeps too long, she'll miss the party."

"We could move the party here," Guy suggested.

Theodore Too thought hard. "But then Macdonald Bridge and George Lighthouse couldn't come. We have to wake Gerta up!"

Hup-hup-hup brrrrrr. Even with Guy flapping his wing against the railing, the ship wouldn't wake up.

"Let's blow our horns together," said Lucy Tug, coming up behind them.

"We could play 'Happy Birthday,'" Theodore Too said.

The two tugboats blew their horns. Guy called out "ice cream" as loud as he could, and even George Lighthouse, inside the harbour, flashed his lights and blew his horn.

Hup-hup-hup brrrrrr, snored Gerta.

"Don't look now," said Theodore Too, "but those are storm clouds forming on the horizon. I think it's going to rain."

Guy Seagull shivered and settled on Theodore Too's cheery red hat. "I hate storms."

Hup-hup-hup-

BOOM! Lightning flashed through the sky. Gerta woke with a start. "Huh? What happened?"

"You forgot to wake up," Theodore Too said, "but don't worry—"

"Happy birthday!" Gerta said, her cheeks red with embarrassment. "Did I miss the party? Oh, I hope I'm not too late."

"Just in time," Theodore Too said.

"For ice cream!" said Guy Seagull.

"Ice cream? Let's go!" said Gerta.

Theodore Too guided his friends back into the harbour while the rain washed everyone clean.

By the time they reached the cake and ice cream, the sun was already peeping out again. Macdonald Bridge, Dartmouth Ferry, George Lighthouse, Lucy Tug, Guy Seagull and Theodore Too finished the day laughing and singing.